infinity plus special editions

HOW MUCH IS THAT MERMAID?

ANNA TAMBOUR

An infinity plus special edition
Published by infinity plus
www.infinityplus.co.uk

ISBN: 978-1-7645172-0-1

Contents

Foreword

Garry Kilworth

HOW MUCH IS THAT MERMAID? is one of those stories where you find yourself slowly immersing in familiarity and yet knowing you're going to be jolted out of it by the end.

A good few of Anna Tambour's stories fill me with unease. I enjoy being uneased, it's what I read fantastical fiction for, but her writing is uniquely eerie, not blatant horror. The scene isn't grisly, but you have an uncomfortable feeling that you're sinking into a perturbant world and you find yourself looking up, peering around the room, making sure that the things that should be still and quiet aren't showing a tendency not to be.

This is one of those tales where foreboding hangs on the edge of every sentence.

How much is that mermaid? is not just about a mythical sea creature, it's about what's happening to the world we live in. It took me to somewhere dark and unexpected.

Fabulous, in the real meaning of the word.

How much is that mermaid?

Anna Tambour

Introduction to 2nd edition, *Vicious Sisters* by
Sirenia Pelagia Weisselbaum

*. . . but like most scientists, her discoveries only would
have led her to more research.*

*This book, and this remarkable woman, tore my
known knowns from my eyes and changed my life so much, I
was honored when she granted me the privilege of giving her
and captaining her mission and taking her name.*

—Shelby "Skipp" Schuyler Weisselbaum,
SMPL, ADS, former Director, The Sargasso
Initiative, co-founder of Compassionate Harvest

High moon, somewhere on the high seas

UNDER THE MAGNIFYING-GLASS focus of an unseasonably friendly September sun, the last of the ice in the window display melted mid-morning. Squirmers the size of drug warnings on meds scrawl s o e s s ~ e ~ ~ over the sequined bling of iridescent scales, origamic fins, teeth like needles, swords, and ears of corn; gold-flecked eyeballs half-hid by lappetted lids; and hair. Aye, hair. No sprigs of parsley, no plastic greenery. Here, exclusively here, mermaid hair in every colour humans can see. Neatly tied ringlets, poufs, and ne'er-forget-me knots, many strands moving. The map-of-the-world pattern on the tasselled wobbegong is crammed with travellers. Squigglers perch on the brows of a stargazer's mistreated-bulldog face. Six-point 's's snake across the cratering vastness of the ratfish's fullmoon eyes.

The fish are merely cats before a queen.

Like the Oscars dress of a nominee the morning after, the extravagant scarlet tailfin of a *Sirena macromastia* splays, reeking of last night's prophylactic lashings of perfume. In this case, that tonka, vanilla and chemical fire accord is not courtesy of say, Kenzo Amour. It's Raid. Her tawny face is poreless, her beauty an uncanny valley of what she must have been. Mouth wrinkles radiate, two so deep, they've cracked. Hard breasts strain the fabulous corset of moonstones, blood coral, and 50 lb, 8-strand braid—models of defiance. She'd only need legs to be a regular at Christie's a short walk away, or (before the partners scarpered) an enrolee of the Tassel Curtain Tie-back workshop at Bows Arts next door.

T HERE COMES A TIME in every relationship when thoughts turn to fantasies.

Getting caught screwing in public by someone who can't do a bloody thing about it. A few weeks away together, bigger boobs, longer prick, hair on head and not on back, or chin. Looking cool together, the getting of a modest shed, a yacht stinking of champagne. Getting an award so important, photographers want a picture of the happy couple. Time away alone. A new life together. A cleaver that'll whack years off Time. And love? It can't be helped that thoughts turn to it like the coils of a spring that are never released, always turning back upon themselves. So "We've got so much love, it's selfish that we don't share it."

"You've met somebody!"

"No."

"Don't lie to me."

"I'm not! It's someone you've known for a long time."

But most fantasies don't escape people's mouths.

In Siren Seafoods, they have included long hair snaring the gullet, pacifisicosa (paralysis of the face caused by eating mermaids sourced from the Challenger Deep), and the suicide-inducing tinnitus of mermaids' mocking sea shanties. Filleting has featured so frequently in his fantasies that he froze his knives in a tray of ice and soaked his pillow with tears the night he punched her nose so good, it crunched like crusted snow under a boot.

This morning before dawn, the two of them had had words—three one-syllable words, impossible to take back.

To look at them now, you'd think they're working too hard to fantasise.

He pours disinfectant into a bucket and plunges the mop in. She leans into the window display, pulling out the contents and dropping them into a wheeled tub, until all that is left is that mummified merm odalisquing on a couch, heavy-lidded eyes looking everyone back through half-cocked horn-rims, a crack-backed copy of *Old Man and the Sea* in perpetual suspension half-sliding off that zaftig sequined lap.

She drags the tub to the door of the walk-in freezer, takes a deep breath, flips open the handle and, checking over her shoulder—he's bent over the mop, working away at something by the swing door to the back hall—viciously kicks the bin in.

The floor cases are next, packed with cuts. Cubes of featureless flesh pink as cupcake icing, yard-long, hairy legs of spider crabs; a goblin shark's head, its snaggletoothed retractable jaw wired into safety position; two brisket cuts of merm hip; three boned merm shanks. She always had to reason with herself about them. She can feel their long muscles through her thick supergrip rubber gloves. Insane. She of all people. Mermaids wrapping their arms around sailors' necks isn't evidence-based, but touching a merm arm triggers childhood memories of wetting the bed rather than braving the arms reaching from behind the toilet, taloned hands clamping her ankles.

The next case is a rococo structure of armoured glass and tortured stainless steel, a fingerprint lock facing the front window. She hasn't opened it for so long, the door sticks. Yeah, nah, the lock is as sham as the cameras and the sign saying "Smile for us. ICU." He won't even have a smart phone in the same room with him. His old friends were the same. Since he lost them, he conveniently lost his phone.

She hears him hitting a back wall's skirting board with the mop head. She needs a stool to reach the glass-fronted cabinet behind the counter, holding the last of the jewellery-box-like trunks. Only two are left, the gorgeous little chased-gold and the larger, flashier crystal-barnacled. Both the suckling and the exclusively mermilk-fed weaner inside have been prepared to the highest standards of legacy, though the sign "You never actually own" disappeared after a nasty letter.

The gold box with the suckling, she slides out and places on the floor. The larger, flashy chest is too unwieldy.

Onwards, to "the movie stars". She opens their six-foot tall display, touches the closest one's cheek, so dewy looking, but as dinner party fare, a gumboot would be more tender. Those three plump faces with their oh so appealing eyes prick tears out of hers. Their sale papers include warnings to remove the eyes if heating, because the glass in others *has* exploded. He calls them the Babes. Their hair is the pale halo, just when the sun takes over from dawn, of the third moult. They're practically *children*.

They probably stink, too. It's impossible to separate any source of scent in the rising fug. The face she touched felt sweaty and slimy, like makeup under klieg lights. Come to think of it, she does, too, not surprising since Scottish Power cut off the juice.

Her face is a study in blue and red, dark hollows and unsymmetrical swells. She straightens up and looks back yet again, wishing she were Lot's wife. It was so quick with her, so painless.

Her imagination flings pictures: her fists breaking glass, her stabbing her stomach with a shard, crushing glass in a fist till her juice runs red as pomegranate, then pouring glass kernels into her

17

mouth; climbing to the roof and jumping off; downing pills—all kinds of iffy stuff. What if it doesn't work, if she's saved before it has the time? Imagining, dreaming, muttering all she dares at the sink while pulling great gobs of rainbow-hued merhair from her sticky gloves. Hair the same colours as her shortcut cap.

The morning he came downstairs just as the shop opened and she surprised him with it. *Hooeey!*

He'd clenched his hands at Hercule and spoke so quietly, the poor guy ran out the back door without so much as one of his rattail combs.

"You allowed Herc to crash on the floor of the shop," she gently reminded Skipp. "You said he was your friend."

"From our Rainbow Warrior days! This is now. You did it to say *Fuck you, Skipp*. What other reason could you have?"

"Your friend was trying to help us. He seems an observer. He was thinking of us. He thought the customers would like it."

She never knew if that was a mistake or self-sabotage. "I hope I'll just be an hour," she said the next day. "An hour," he reminded her.

She'd looked up wig places and had to pick the closest. A Shakespearean actress type practically shoved her out the door with a "Dearie, they'll take care of you at Shelter. The thirty-four bus. Or, here, let's get you a taxi." And the woman prepaid the ride. Shelter, a stalwart of the op-ed district, did indeed have many used mops, as well as a tragic number of used dog beds. It could have been kinda ironical fun trying wigs on like so many hats, everyone politely averting their gaze from the bald patches—decidedly not due to cancer treatment—if she'd had time. She made it back to the shop/home with three minutes to spare on his pre-battery watch.

Another mistake was presenting him with the bag of her cut glory. A pound and a half of natural dreadlocks that had reached past her waist. Black as twenty-thousand leagues under the sea, and famously lit with fairy lights in that *Nat Geo* cover feature, "MIND, BODY, WONDER: Six scientists ponder why they're judged so sexy."

Not that he could talk. He was one of the six. The gilded half-naked god, sea-beaded hair jewelling his arms. He's now the blotched jaundice yellows of a supermarket custard tart, and his graceful slouch has changed to one of furtive shoplifter, but he can't hide his shopkeeper's paunch.

From the way he's swabbing the handcut mosaic of that floor, you could think the rental agent dragon herself will be coming through the door.

Its bell jangles.

"We're closed," Sirenia says.

"At two o'clock? Come, now."

She doesn't turn around. Pulling merhair from the sticky grip of her non-slip gloves, a long sour mess dangles from her right hand. She'd been pondering flinging it to the floor.

"And sure if I've not got a wee bit on my plate as well, darlin'."

The swabbing stops. Skipp steps forward.

"Sorry for the inconvenience, miss. The lady's right. We'll open at nine-thirty tomorrow."

"It's not your delicacies I'd be after, wouldn't you know?"

"Then if you don't mind . . ." He does this generous bow and flourish thing that had been such a popular part of his schtick.

"I do at that."

She steps forward. "Sorry," she says firmly.

"No need to apologise. And such a pretty sight you are, standing by your man." The visitor's fingers twiddle like a crooked landlord's in an antique cartoon, and two cards fan out from between slim fingers. "Youse called. Take."

Sirenia Pelagia Weisselbaum shrugs, takes one, looks at it and loses her balance. The mop crashes as her husband/partner grabs her left arm. Her wet right hand crushes the card till its print, **Angel of Murder**, is easy to read as tea leaves in a compost heap.

"We're not looking for a decorator," she says. "And I'd advise you to cut the plastic Emerald Isle patter and don't even try an och aye."

"Sir," says the visitor, shoving the other card forward.

Luckily, Skipp hates being pushed. Sirenia leans in, flicks the card onto the wet floor and treats it like a cockroach.

"Discretion," says the visitor to Serenia, tapping the side of his nose.

"Didn't you hear her?" The blue of Skipp's eyes has gone choppy grey.

Sirenia clucks. "It must be the wellness clinic," she says to Skipp. "But Roman skipped months ago."

She steps to the door and reaches around to the small of the visitor's back. *Her* back faces *him*. "Nobody left on this block, I'm afraid." She hopes her eyes are legible. Just three simple words: *Please fuck off.*

"Roman, you say?" says the visitor. "I do apologise. I'm just following an old lead. A thousand thank youses."

"HUMANS." Skipp's got one hand around the mop's back, poised to dance. "You believe her story."

"What? No."

"Why was she lying? Why'd you give her cover? Don't you see what she was doing? No one ever sees."

"What was she doing?"

"What do you *think* she was doing?"

"I don't know. She's a decorator."

"Why'd you think that?"

"Her card."

"You believe cardboard?" Bubbles form on the floor around the mop head, he's pushing down so hard. "She was *casing* the place! You might as well have tossed her the keys."

"Our mermaids are too distinctive to be—"

"Not them, you dumb fuck. The chandelier. You should know. You're the people person."

Her right hand is digging nails into her left arm, away from his sight. *She?* The visitor was a good six-foot-five of wiry muscle with a neat blonde beard and the duck-bum posture of a cyclist.

"Fuuck!" he screams, throwing the mop against the swing door to the back. "She *was* beautiful, no?"

"Mm."

"You didn't answer the phone earlier, did you?"

"I told you I wouldn't."

"That's no answer. Why are you being like this? Why?"

"I'm not being like anything."

"You're doing it *again!*"

"I was agreeing with you."

23

"Why do you always disagree?"

"With what? Please tell me."

"Just get out. Get *out!*"

"Yes."

"What?"

"Yes. I didn't mean to."

"Then why do you?"

"*Why . . . do . . . you . . . always . . . argue!*"

"I'm sorry. I don't mean to . . ."

"Shut up!"

ASIDE FROM SOME UNEVEN breathing, the only sounds in here are the drips of taps and drains. The mosquito whine of lights, the dull heartthrobs of refrigeration generators. They're gone with the ice, victims of computer-controlled pay policing.

Sirenia is crouched behind the counter, curled against the wall. The floor around her is a landscape of red deltas. She breathes through her mouth because her nostrils are filled with blood's rusted-iron clots. Her crotch and thighs wear the cold compress of her own shit. Her bum is hard as a hospital pillow, but her arms floppy with tenderised muscles. To her left is the treasure chest holding the suckling in the treasure chest that she hadn't known what to do with: smash or hide.

He finds her, reaches a hand down and pulls her up. "Sore?"

"A bit." She smiles at him with her lips, molars clenched from the strain of not jerking herself away. "Beans on toast?"

"Anything."

"She *was* beautiful," he says. "No?"

"She was."

"You were too hasty. She *might* have been a customer. When was the last time we had one? Did you pay the rent?"

"No," she lies. "I took your point. I haven't."

"You haven't found anyone to keep Lola till we're settled?"

"Not yet."

"So much for your friends."

Her nails rake raw thighs. What about *your* friends? Where is precious Kiril, who you paid a fortune to, and Kevin K, and that guy from Greenland? Actually, all your fine seamates from Novosibirsk to Makassar? All pre-pay mateship.

25

"Want help climbing the stairs?"

"Thanks. I'll manage."

An hour later, they're screwing like a Kansas twister. (No, that last bit is a fib that only happens in fiction. Each left the shop by the elegant Georgian door, slipped around the corner of the listed building, entered its dark architectural arsehole, and made their way up steep stairs to the flat where first, she slapped together a Vegemite sandwich, placing it on the upturned milk carton beside his chair along with a folded paper towel and a note she'd scrawled—Will be out of toilet soon—ending with a scrawled heart.

She stripped in the shower stall, her load turning her panties inside out as an overripe fig. There followed a period of furtive release—hissed whispers, barefoot kicks, choked gasps half-muffled by the petulant bangs of the ad hoc, stressed-out plumbing.

All too soon, the hot runs out. She snatches the sodden leather belt she'd hung from the HOT, and whips the floor of the DIY discount tray base so hard, the buckle cracks it open, exposing a few flabby fibreglass muscles.

Shivering and dripping, *I hate this life, I hate this life*, streams out of her mouth in a scream of a rasp between bouts of biting her hands, pounding her thighs. *I hate this life* streaming till all the words flow together—a shitstream of words falling on the deaf, broken floor while the shower flows, frigid as the North Sea..

Words. The place stinks of words. "That's *it*," she mumbles. *It*. Grief hurts most at the bottom of the swallow well. The physical pain is a wet blanket wrapping her as she sits on the throne itself.

His boots on the gritty, uncarpeted stairs. No time to move.

"Are you alright," he says, peeking around the door.

"Just having a bout of the runs."

"Righto. Thank you for the sandwich. You must eat too."

"I will," she says. "I'll be in there soon."

"Okay,"

"Like fuck okay," she whispers when she can hear the TV.

He likes her to sit with him when he watches.

WAITING IN A CLEARED space on her chairside table is a steaming cup of dirty chai.

"Thank you," she says.

"Anything for you, m'lady."

Rituals.

They're statues, eyes forward, for maybe an hour. "Want to talk?" he says, manually turning it off.

"If you do."

"If *you* do. If you're going to make some sense."

"I'll try." There's so much *to* talk about, and so little. Life coming to the end of its string, she wants to say, and doesn't. Maybe doesn't dare. Maybe doesn't care enough to dare.

"You never want to face anything," he says.

"That's true."

"Have you even tried to make any plans?"

"Not successfully."

"Well, you're the people person. This move was *your* idea."

"Mm."

"What?"

"Yes, it was," she says. "And I agree, it isn't working out."

"It's not all your fault. You can never depend on people. They *say* they want something but they don't. They say the weather will be sunny or the el nino's last year's mess. And they lie to us. And you with your assessment of high ends. Maybe if you hadn't drifted away. We used to do everything together."

"We still do."

"What's that supposed to mean?"

"I'll try harder."

"Are you sore?" He reaches out and rubs her back. "Wanna massage?"

"It just hurts when I laugh," she laughs. Her molars are so cracked, the nerves are live wires.

"Want to watch a couple hours before bed?"

"Sure."

For the next hour, she keeps her eyes on the screen while marvelling at life, its curious matings. Who would have thought that the hedgehog cunt is impregnable without brute force? Who could have guessed this street of all locations in this town of foreigners burdened with too much wealth would have a major unfixable sewer leak that is death for business?

Who could have seriously imagined that the true story of the mermaids and their oddly sustainable catch would have fallen on uncaring ears?

People are just cant. No one cared enough to support their compassionate capture and snapdry or -freeze technology that this one outlet in the world could boast of. Why did people misbelieve the truth about mermaids, a species more vicious than wolves any day? A society that expels so many young ones to suffer a cruel, lonely death in grottos mermaids built so long ago, naturalists view these torture chambers as natural? Why do people who say they care not give a fuck about compassionate eating? Why do they need irony, snobbery, astronomical prices to value something, only to flick that care away the next moment like a shirt from Zara.

And who knew that the month life turned into shit creek itself, sparked by unsympathetic drive-by pieces everywhere from the *Guardian* to RT, he would come down with something going around and lose his sense of smell? Lucky, eh? That and a bad case of farsightedness allowed the place to go to ruin under his nose and eyes, not that they'd had a walk-in customer for donks. He'd taken to swabbing the floor to keep busy. Rent? Fuckit, he said. He'd never dealt with the bills or bank, only the suppliers of their most edgy stuff, who she always paid up front because those kind of people don't trust nobody.

So when the doorbell jangled that afternoon, she thought it might be Deodorant, the learner bloke from the rental agency. Still, he had to be got rid of asap. Thus, the rudeness. But who sent the prankster? And why the awful Irish twaddle?

Skipp chuckles, a familiar one-syllable laugh. "Idiots. That's an American Bradley, not a Russian T55's ass. And Kalashnikov wasn't an inventor. He was a manufactured hero. No?" he barks.

"Wha? No." She's developed a brain-replay that doesn't engage any other part of her grey matter.

"I shouldn't watch these with you."

"I agree with you about Kalashnikov."

"And not about the tanks?"

"Yes. I didn't catch—"

"Why do they use these things. Do they think we're stupid? They must. You didn't see."

Halfway through the next program, he turns it off midscene and walks to the kitchen sink. That's the sign the evening's entertainment is over. She shrugs and gets up too.

He's already drinking a glass of water when she hands him his pills.

"Is this right?" he says, examining them.

"Yes," she says. He downs the cup of them and goes to the loo where she can hear him first, having a pee, then starting his elaborate toothbrushing routine.

She grabs her own toothbrush from a tumbler on the counter and accidentally stabs her gums with it. The cold stone sink invites. It's been the death of dishes. Her favourite knife, an 8-inch Global, glints at her from the wall. The wooden stairs beckon in her memory. Slippery despite their grot, they're so narrow and swaybacked with age, they could be brilliant killers, *but what if I only fall wrong, only manage to cut my head, break a leg?*

She wipes her face on a towel grey and shiny as salmon skin.

Finally, he flushes. She waits another minute before going to have a pee herself.

Her every breath hurts as she bends down to kiss him in the double bed where he's placed himself so close to this edge, she'd have three quarters of it.

He reaches for a tit. "Wanna cuddle?"

"Thanks. I think I just need to sleep."

He pulls the doona up to his neck and turns his back to her. "We'll leave tomorrow morning," he says. "I'll pack. You're getting the tickets from your travel agent friend, no?"

Iwoma Janikowski. She was Siren Seafoods' first real customer. Came in out of curiosity, left with a heart broken by the lives of those poor mermaids. *She* certainly wanted to help. She spent a fortune on a whole merm, talking of some Polish specialty she planned for her son's wedding, a feature dish with homemade aspic. A week later, she brought photos of it into the shop. Sirenia agreed, quite honestly, that the dish did them proud, especially the traditional headpiece, a crown of carrots and celery. Candelabras on both ends of the long platter, the merm floating in clear aspic with grasslike pieces of green onion lightly lapping her sides, looked a cross between Ophelia and a queen on a funeral barge. "She was delicious," Iwoma had said.

"Hey, the travel agent. The tickets."

"I said I would get them."

"We haven't seen her for a while."

True. Iwoma had given Sirenia every chance, grasping her hands when his back was turned. Few people made Sirenia feel guilty, but Iwoma *had*. Sirenia had politely refused every invitation to visit the woman at home or work. "No time," was her excuse. Not entirely untrue. "Silverknowes?" he'd said. "Where the fuck is that?"

It wasn't just claustrophobia the woman induced in Sirenia but alarm. In her presence, Sirenia felt as transparent as a glass eel. She had no idea what the softhearted, passionate Pole might do.

One painful night, Sirenia looked Krakow Travel up. Its site was on sale from Go Daddy. She wasn't surprised. Who uses travel agents anymore?

"She's probably busy."

"Take a bus," he says. "It's too far to walk."

"Okay." She kisses his ear. "Sleep well."

Mouthing *You have no idea,* she turns off the overhead bulb. The travel agent that doesn't exist anymore, paid with money they don't have anymore.

"Hey," he says. "Why do we still have electricity up here?"

"Domestic account. They have to issue more notices."

She turns off the light and pads down the gritty gap-boarded hall to the spare room. It's easy to find the way. In this town, it must be illegal to curtain windows. The old buildings of New Town possess a pale, supremely confident elegance, like Liz the First's smooth face—all high forehead and cold, lashless eyes. The passersby are expected to respectfully look aside. But come night, when the lights indoors are out, all these stonefaced buildings stare out, gouged blind, while the soul of the town scrapes every cranny's secrets with its streetlights.

The single bed in the spare room rises above an ocean of kit, gear, and books. Streetlight pouring into the window catches the mound of Miflex Xtreme regulator hoses looking so like a yellow-bellied sea snake orgy, they could have been posed by Gordon Entwhistle, the frustrated would-be standup comic who'd created Lola's bustier. There's no wardrobe or laundry basket here, or system as such, but the dirtiest clothes are piled in one corner.

In the same strong Dewar's carton as that sentimental keepsake, the specimen jar holding the first abused merm she'd ever saved, is Wiley's first edition of *The Aetiology of Psychopathic Social Systems in Sirenic Communities* by Sirenia Pelagia Weisselbaum, the spark that lit their romance.

IN FOETAL POSITION, SHE'S been "sleeping" with her ears so strained, she's triggered one of the off-key voices.

> *Sailor sailor, drink your tipple*
> *from my unctuousest nipple.*
> *And should you die afore you'd wake*
> *you lucky dog,*
> *for I've snatched your snake.*
> *Yo ho! I've got your snake.*

So my teeth are false, 'Tis oh so true.
That detail didn't bother you.
You're mine, you said,
grabbing me by the head.
Sailor, oh, sailor.

Sailor, sailor,
my teeth in a glass, your snake in their grasp.
I've got your snake in my looking glass.
Sailor sailor, lost your todger?
Semaphore for a new pants lodger.

Sailor sailor . . .

HER BED SHAKES. "Don't worry," he says. "I'm not going to hurt you. Wanna talk?"

"Uh?" She rubs her face, hard, aping sleep befuddlement.

"Let's leave tomorrow morning," he says. "I'll pack and you get the tickets from that travel agent friend of yours."

"Aye."

"Cash, remember? Did I take my pills?"

"Yes."

"And you *still* haven't thought about Lola."

"I've had many thoughts. I might have an idea."

"Too late." He reels away.

Ears *do* strain. Hers hardly need to. His inhuman scream when he reaches the bedroom would wake the neighbours if there were any left. It does set off a dog.

She's hyperawake. Not knowing if he's going to come in again or not is only part of it.

Lola. Leaving her behind hurts almost as much as giving in to the demands of irony had. She'd had one seriously fucked-up life, but to spend it in perpetuity as some burlesque fantasy to half-smirk at. Why?

Lola, national clickbait when the couple had to flee from Martha's Vineyard.

But Boston could have been worse, Sirenia had had to explain to Skipp because he just didn't *see* it. When Americans turn on you, it's 360 degrees. "That makes no sense," he'd said.

"One hundred eighty then. The opposite direction, I mean."

"You don't know what you mean. Just shut up."

"I know it's not logical, but—"

"Shut up!"

In the Martha's Vineyard shop, he'd draped a white scarf modestly over Lola's breasts, and placed her standing, not lolling, on a classic white pedestal, so the outrage was all the greater over her supposed mistreatment because she couldn't be slutshamed.

Skipp was his old self for a few weeks. Serenia got the full knightly schtick. He called her m'lady, made her tea, massaged her feet, and late one Saturday night, ran her a bath, lit a candle, poured her a glass of something way too expensive, and closed the door. She drank up and fell asleep, her head cradled on the perfumed towel he'd placed just so.

The water was lukewarm when he woke her, helped her out and put her to bed. He got in too, exhausted but electrically awake, having used her time in the bath to pack.

SKIPP MANAGED TO GET Lola out with them, too, when they left the States for a life Serenia had no clue of, nor did she ask his plans.

She was too hurt, too numb, to do anything but float. His old Sea Shepherd best mate had suggested the destination, and Edinburgh was at first, refreshing. No morals to speak of. The shop was cheap as chips to lease. The next door neighbours, Bows Arts, were more welcoming than Scots, probably because they were from Brighton and the East End (of London, Jules explained). Gordon designed and constructed Lola's corset himself. Gordon's partner Jules sourced the most amazing chandelier. He said it had hung in Catherine the Great's bedroom. By the third week, Siren's Seafoods had to place queue ropes and bollards in the shop, there were so many prospective customers. Mostly Russians—the only problem with them: they came to haggle.

Skipp was so ingratiatingly polite, all *sir* this, *sir* thatting to every customer till one rude turd was so obviously having him on, she wanted to puke, but laughed, taking the fun from the turd's tease, so he left in a huff.

Once the door jangled shut, Skipp turned on her. "What was that for, Seer?"

"What?"

The shop shut early that day.

But after that first rush, those *mudaks*, as he called them, put his nose out of joint. That's when he inadvertently taught her the Russian for "Take your eyes out of your arsehole", "Go to Tesco's", and "Your mother should have shoved a peach pit up her twat". He'd banter with the Poles who pitched up to buy ratfish. He'd joke and then kick out with laughing insults the students on exchange from the University of Bologna who viewed the shop as a free museum. He was only genuinely rude to those Russians who treated him like some blind babushka pickle seller ripe for outcheating.

"A waste," Sirenia had told him often back in Martha's Vineyard, a town where at any moment, the next customer could be the President ushering in a supposed world leader for a photo op. She'd be roped into them—she and her famous hair and the boobs so round and perfect, they'd earned her the moniker Dugong, then Dugs before she took to masking them under her first adult judo jacket, an *uwagi* so old, it was ripped as designer-stressed jeans. There were other hyperfamous customers then, but many were likely to be camera-shy day trippers who'd coptered in off yachts bigger than most islands. Some spoke English. Many didn't but they'd heard of the place, and of course, Skipp. He had more languages than a farmed salmon, parasites, but they came so naturally, he didn't respect people who thought just knowing them worth letters. His only PhD relating to Russia itself was the one from Brown, that dissertation *Costs of Compassion: A study of the history of Nature interfering with Russian social direction, from The Tale of Ihor's Campaign to the global Freezer Fleet strategy in the 9th Five-Year Plan* by Shelby T. Schuyler.

Those were good times, so busy that she stopped keeping up with both Itakura at NENV and that dear sentimental earthmother-oceanographer, Nezrin Ozturk, who reached out to her from Project PERSEUS. Itakura really did die—that she confirmed. But did Nezrin's daughter Canan lie when she said Nezrin doesn't recognise anyone, that Alzheimer's scrambled her brain? Sirenia never could find out, cut off from everyone—every body, association, even informal chat group. And phones? She'd been lucky to talk to Nezrin's daughter who still had a landline in the old family home and never kept up with scandals. Alzheimer's—*the paranoia might be unpleasant, but anything that can erase the present can't be bad.*

THAT SHAKING OF THE bed, again. Ever so lightly, breathe out. Then in—

"Don't worry." Not *his* voice. She sneaks a peek, and crikey, it's the visitor. A man alright, starkers, perched on the foot of her bed. She should be terrified but he's fuzzy and warm as a puppy. She wriggles her left foot free.

"Pardon me," he says.

"How'd you get here?" she whispers. "We've no lock to speak of, but the stairs—"

"So you want to talk about stairs?"

She sits up and pulls up the covers. But he hasn't closed the door and Skipp *can't* be sleeping.

"He can't hear us."

"How would you know?"

He cocks an eyebrow. "Who do you take me for?" He's looking for something, doesn't find it. "There isn't a spare chair under this mess, is there?"

The fake brogue has gone. "Tell you right. Let's go somewhere you like, a place conducive to discussion. That place with the mossy chairstones by the Water of Leith?"

"No. Please no. Merms—" She had loved the walk by that strangely named river running through Edinburgh, so close that when new in town, she had escaped there for a few minutes every now and then. The rippling green light under the beech, ash, and wych elms, the sibilance of leaves—until one day, she heard another sound. An offkey, offbeat sing-song, a cruel giggle, and a splash. In the old days of mere study, she'd have logged it as a sighting.

But the way the waters roiled with laughter confirmed: this is no sighting; *it's a stalking*.

"Shh, shh," the Angel of Murder says, stroking her head. "Get dressed. We'll work out where on the way."

"Hand me something from there," she says.

"Hardly."

He piggybacks her silently and smoothly through wall and cloud. The air is nippy but he's so warm, not at all like the beach he deposits her on.

"Scotland and beaches," he says in a kind of apology.

The stones, cold and wet as a dungeon, dig into her tenderised bum. Beside her, a ball of snarled fishing line glistens like a merm's scalped hair, one hook slyly protruding. Her right hand, steadying her on the stones, jerks away from something sharp. The knife-edge of a shard of blue-willow plate.

"Finished?" he says. "Why?"

"Why what?"

"Don't be coy now. I can leave."

"It's too complicated."

"Everything always is. Time is lives."

"So we met at a sustainability summit in Bruges."

"Good start. Now go on."

He tosses her something that looks like a red velvet cape but scoots under her bum like a warm wet sea cucumber.

"I needed to escape," she says, nodding a thank you. "I never wanted to be famous. Just wanted a way to save them. Everyone else just exploits. Compassionate Harvest is *his* concept. I could only think as far as saving them somehow, but then what? He got us out of the grant merry-go-round. Sure, he kept his positions in both NOAH and the Sea Shepherd Foundation but was finished with begging, he said."

"Didn't that book of yours make you a millionaire?"

"You know about that? Do you know what science costs? And science is nothing compared to the costs of compassionate harvest. Everything went into costs. He's not very good with money, you know. Even that merm that the president of Mexico bought. It brought us no real profit because we had loans to service and the overheads of the harvest are astronomical. Gold extraction is cheaper. All the money from that book, *all* the money, I poured into harvesting. So when the shit hit the fan, I even lost my agent.

"But surely, royalties?"

"I've been told I'm lucky the publishers don't sue me for the cost of pulping my books."

"My condolences. Cry away. I'm here for you."

"Ta. We did great that first year. We'd not only been saving traumatised mermaids slated for cruel deaths, but through instant, painless euthanasia, could bring the catch to tables around the world as the first truly guiltless luxuries for vegans who miss meat on principle."

"So what went wrong?"

"You really *don't* know?"

The angel's shoulders twitch. "You *are* important to us, but."

"Sex. America. Sex to Americans. *The Intercept* led, reporting that the Icelandic skipper of one of our ships wasn't just rescuing but abusing. It only took less than a day for us to get hit with mermaid trafficking headlines so bad, Martha's Vineyard City Council slapped a notice on our door. All our stock would have been impounded too, if it weren't for agency border wars and *his* connections. We were never charged with anything, you know. We never knew anything about that stuff they reported. It was a giant smear."

"A smear?"

"Jealousy. Probably some woman Skipp rebuffed. Or someone trying to get into the trade. He designed the processing to my specs. Painless. Compassionate. That's the whole—"

"Alright. So then?"

"His connections got us to Aberdeen. A suckhole."

"But you set up in Edinburgh with great fanfare, I saw from the writeups."

"So you *have* researched."

"A bit."

"Then you must know we were toast of the town. National pride loves moral superiority."

"Then why did you jettison that fabulous name, Compassionate Harvest?"

"It's Oxfam. Everyone here said. You see anyone feasting on Oxfam turkeys? Of course not. Oxfam is all about death to extravagance. It's anti-indulgence. It's penitential woollens and sawdust-textured oatcakes, with dog-hair on everything. Compassionate Harvest is all about compassionately, *lovingly*, having your indulgence and eating it too. But the meaning of compassion here has been poisoned, so it had to be jettisoned."

"Still, you should have made a success, the two of you."

"We were quite the couple. You know he took my name?"

"I know." He's picking his nails with a fishbone.

"Sorry."

"No probs. But the problem is, I *am* quite busy. Can we get on with it? Dawn is rather bruising the old sky."

"I wish you hadn't reminded me. I must get back."

"To what?" he snaps, "Why?"

She rolls on her knees to stand up, but the cold stones dig into her kneecaps and her muscles won't obey. And the sun isn't playing kind. "Look," she says. "You're very sweet to come, but I can't murder my way to making a viable business."

"Young lady, I deserve some respect. You can jettison the insouciance right this moment. You've been spending half your waking hours fantasising about topping yourself."

"So?"

"So who do you think I am? A lawyer?"

"Not dressed like that. Can't you see, the business is finished? We're skint but he doesn't know it?"

"Business! No business is worth that. And it's so common. You're not common, are you?"

"I hope not."

"So pooh on business. Has he always been violent? You can tell me. Is it Scotland's water?"

"No."

"So you've now lied to the limit of viable life."

"You could say that."

"What is your order? If you'd like my suggestion, drowning would be so poe—"

"No! Have you ever seen a bycatch curled in death paroxysm? Have you any idea the grip a mermaid has on a shipwrecked sailor? I was thinking, being hit by a bus."

"How inconsiderate. And how will he cope without you? Have you thought of that?"

"That's the only reason I haven't."

Her flippant face folds into a crumpled mess.

"Seer," says the angel. "You like being called Seer?"

"It's better than Dugs."

"No time for private jokes. Under the guidelines, I could help you, but murdering you would be such a waste. You've still got a life to live."

"As what?"

"I'm serious."

"You honestly think so?"

"I could get you to one of those grottos you discovered, where you can live with those poor expelled mermaids."

"Hell, no!"

"You would care for them."

"Hell no, on skis! They're psycho! You misunderstand, too. The whole *point* of Compassionate Harvest is saving them by preserving the memory of *what they could have been, but never had a chance.* Our Quickfreeze and Quickdry processes have made sure they—"

"So I take it you don't wish to spend the rest of your life rehabilitating damaged mermaids?"

"Irrevocably damaged mermaids. Over my dead body."

"It's such a waste of murder."

"What other choice do I have? I have some dignity left, and would rather die painlessly. He's gonna beat me to death, probably as soon as I get back."

"Yet you never managed to think ahead and do the deed. Are they merely fantasies? Here, let's stand up." He proffers her a crisp paper towel. "Blow your nose."

"You can't do better than that?"

"I'm only the Angel of Murder. So why haven't you done it already? Would you like to hear my theory? He's too helpless."

"So you *do* know. He needs me."

"Convenient for him. This escape. What are his plans?"

"Crewing for his old friend, Baldur Hrund. Baldur's son won't do it. He's a cryptobanker in London."

"How does he know Baldur wants him?"

"The feeling, he says. Hey, I don't know how Skipp could have mistaken you for some hot babe."

"Easy. I am to each of you, what you make of me."

"Really?"

"Cross my heart."

"You're not lying to me?"

"I respect you too much for that. What? Are you laughing or crying?"

"I don't know."

"You really would be *such* a waste."

"Such a waste, such a waste. You some goddamn parrot?"

"Remember your words today? Were they yours or his?"

"His. Mine. I don't remember."

"So you aren't making him any more happy than he's making you."

"You could say that."

"I just did. I do have a toofer, just for this sort of thing."

"Huh?"

"Two for one. I could do both of you . . . Oy, what you looking at? Oh, *that*. Dawn breaking over the Forth Bridge. Beyond words, isn't it? Take your time."

"D ON'T WORRY," HE SAYS. "I'll take care of everything. So glad you didn't choose the twofer. I hate waste."

W HAT A BLAST! The whole row went up— whoosh—every listed building in its beautiful decrepitude. The lot of them here one moment, dust the next—in one town-shaking eruption, leaving, where proud Georgian models of modernity had stood almost straight, a gaping canyon. A hole stinking of arse.

The coverage of the actual explosion was a loop of CGI reconstructions, for the CCT was a writeoff. But that day no one could miss the sirens. They yowled so loud, two ghosts in Edinburgh Castle fled. The Headless Drummer, in thoughtless terror, and The Grey Lady, disgusted by the rude awakening from her beauty sleep. As for the explosion, a methane leak, Radio Capital was first to report.

The Comhairle Baile Dhùn Èideann convened an extraordinary session, there was so much blame needing to be apportioned.

She'd stocked up that momentous day. New phone, laptop, clothes fit to be seen in. A surprising amount of dosh. No tickets yet, because no plans. Closure was better, till she could think. She's splayed on a bed at a comfortable hotel, nothing as flash as when she was famous, but this one's impersonal. Time to call room service? She could have, but her gut is a problem. Fluttery, gassy, bloated, out of sorts.

The news cycle for that story has slowed to a stop. It twirled like a mad thing for weeks—listed building, city neglect, development opportunity—spectacular explosion. She watched, listened, read everything, sifting for that one kernel, death. She couldn't have missed it. Had it been hidden away? *Is everyone being lied to?*

Her heart says they aren't. Her head says she's right because if there had been a casualty, even so much as a wee terrier who'd never bark again, there'd be enough outrage to spark a new opposition party.

So a human? And *that* human?

Edinburgh would be infested with photographing news crews. There'd be nowhere to hide.

Her bruises are fading and she can sit anyhow now. The flutters in her gut are something else, and nothing she can see anyone about. They've done it again: set off the singing in her ears.

She leans over on the bed and carefully places her glass of bubbly on the nightstand. Time to open a fresh bag of crisps.

It's a lovely day outdoors. She can see that from the Live Scotland feed streaming on Facebook.

The phone rings. Inconvenient, with her hands and mouth full.

"Thanks," she says, spitting a crisp. "I don't need housekeeping."

"Hello, Miss Smith," says some AI trainer. "We like to keep in touch with our longer-term guests, and there seems to be a wee problem with your card. Could you pop in to the front desk, please."

Hell. On. Skis. Skipp was right about one thing. You can't trust *anyone*.

infinity plus special editions

www.infinityplus.co.uk

www.ingramcontent.com/pod-product-compliance
Lightning Source LLC
Chambersburg PA
CBHW020320150626
46552CB00022B/3018